There's a Fighter in My Room

There's a Fighter in My Room

Megan Kjarbo

Penny Weber

gatekeeper press

Columbus, Ohio

There's a Fighter in My Room

Published by Gatekeeper Press
2167 Stringtown Rd, Suite 109
Columbus, OH 43123-2989
www.GatekeeperPress.com

ISBN (hardcover): 9781642377118
eISBN: 9781642377125
Library of Congress Control Number: 2019945522

It was bedtime, but Matthew could not go to sleep.
"Oh my gosh! There's a fighter in my room!"
It was big and silent and waiting to attack!

Quietly, Matthew tiptoed
out of his room.
Maybe his brother
would save him.

"Jon, come quick! There's a fighter in my room!"

"Is it big?" Jon asked, yawning.

"Yes, with long legs!" says Matthew.

"Is it ugly?" teased Jon.

"Yes!" said Matthew.

"Is it good at hiding?" Jon asked

"Yes!"

"I am a little too small to fight a fighter that big! Why not ask Dad?"
And with that Jon slammed his door shut.

Next, Matthew found his father
in the living room.
"Daddy, come quick! There's a big, ugly
fighter hiding in my room with long legs!"

"Is it a fast fighter?" Matthew's dad asked.

"Yes, he is!" Matthew said. "And he is too high for me to catch!"

"Well, it's a little late now, and I need to take out the garbage and then go to bed. I can help you fight in the morning."

"But I cannot sleep until we take care of him!"
Matthew demanded.

"Then see if your mom can help you," his dad said, and went back to snoozing in his armchair.

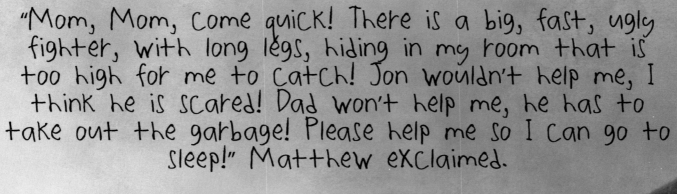

"Mom, Mom, come quick! There is a big, fast, ugly fighter, with long legs, hiding in my room that is too high for me to catch! Jon wouldn't help me, I think he is scared! Dad won't help me, he has to take out the garbage! Please help me so I can go to sleep!" Matthew exclaimed.

"Let's go take care of it,"
she said calmly, rolling up her sleeves.

She grabbed a cup,

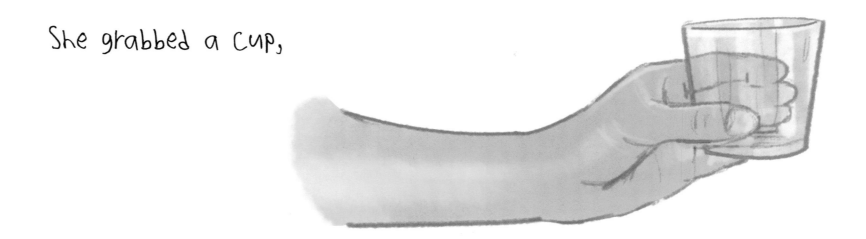

She grabbed a book,

and she picked Matthew up and walked
into his room, with the big, fast, ugly
fighter with long legs that was hiding
too high for Matthew to catch.

"Now where is he?" Matthew's mom asked as she placed Matthew in his bed. He promptly pulled the covers over his head, and pointed.

Matthew's mom approached
the fighter cautiously

trapped it
between
the glass
and the
book...

and walked it to the window and put it outside.

"Bye, spider," she said.

She pulled the covers over Matthew, kissed his forehead, and said goodnight.

CPSIA information can be obtained at www.ICGtesting.com
Printed in the USA
BVIW122134260919
559387BV00015B/95